792.   Gregory, Cynthia
8092

Gre   Cynthia Gregory
dances Swan Lake

14.95

DATE DUE			
DEC 3 1993			
MAR 1 1994			

792.   Gregory, Cynthia
8092

Gre   Cynthia Gregory
dances Swan Lake

14.95

DATE DUE	BORROWER'S NAME	
DEC 3 1993	Rachel. L.	5
EB 2 8 1994	Tina N	5
MAR 1 1994	Tina N	5
MAR 0 9 1994	Jennifer	5
		5

Cynthia Gregory
Dances Swan Lake

Cynthia Gregory Dances Swan Lake

BY CYNTHIA GREGORY

PHOTOGRAPHS BY MARTHA SWOPE

A TIME OF MY LIFE BOOK

SIMON AND SCHUSTER BOOKS FOR YOUNG READERS
PUBLISHED BY SIMON & SCHUSTER INC.
NEW YORK • LONDON • TORONTO • SYDNEY • TOKYO • SINGAPORE

SIMON AND SCHUSTER BOOKS FOR YOUNG READERS
Simon & Schuster Building, Rockefeller Center
1230 Avenue of the Americas, New York, New York 10020
Text copyright © 1990 by Cynthia Gregory
Photographs copyright © 1990 by Martha Swope
All rights reserved including the right
of reproduction in whole or in part in any form.
SIMON AND SCHUSTER BOOKS FOR YOUNG READERS
is a trademark of Simon & Schuster Inc.

All photographs by Martha Swope except for
page 6 by Avenue Studio; page 8 by Al Stainback;
page 9 copyright © 1956 by Bob Willoughby, used by permission of the photographer
and *Dance Magazine;* and page 10 by Pace Publications.

Designed by Sylvia Frezzolini
Manufactured in the United States of America

10   9   8   7   6   5   4   3   2   1

Library of Congress Cataloging-in-Publication Data
Gregory, Cynthia. Cynthia Gregory dances Swan Lake.
Summary: Text and photographs follow leading ballerina Cynthia
Gregory on the day she dances Swan Lake.   1. Gregory, Cynthia –
Juvenile literature.   2. Ballet dancers – United States – Biography –
Juvenile literature.   3. Swan Lake (Ballet) – Juvenile literature.
[1. Gregory, Cynthia.   2. Ballet dancers.   3. Swan Lake (Ballet)]
I. Swope, Martha, ill.   II. Title.   III. Title: Cynthia Gregory dances
Swan Lake. GV1785.G713A3   1990   792.8′092 – dc20
[B]   [92]   89-48018
ISBN 0-671-68786-7

TO LLOYD

One of my very first memories is of being lifted high in the air in the strong arms of my uncle—striking a pretty pose, giggling, and touching the ceiling—while classical music played on the radio. When he put me down, I would dance around my grandmother's living room and dip into a deep bow as the music ended. That was dancing! Moving in response to the music, soaring aloft, and finishing to the delighted applause of family and friends—in a way, that's still what dancing means to me today, after almost thirty years on the stage. At that moment when I'm lifted high at the end of a ballet and the audience is already starting to applaud, I sometimes still recapture the excitement I felt as a four-year-old.

I suppose it is the music, more than anything else, that makes me dance. When I hear music—almost any kind—I can't sit still.

The music composed by Tchaikovsky for *Swan Lake* is one of the most hauntingly beautiful ballet scores ever written. I sometimes feel that Tchaikovsky wrote the music especially for me—even though he wrote it more than seventy years before I was born. It is the music that has kept my performances of *Swan Lake* fresh and new through two decades.

Choreographed in Russia in 1894 by Marius Petipa and his assistant, Lev Ivanov, *Swan Lake* is a wonderful fairy tale. It is the story of Prince Siegfried, who meets Odette, the Swan Queen, and falls in love at first sight. Changed into swans by the evil Von Rothbart, Odette and the swan maidens can only be freed from the spell by a pledge of eternal love. Siegfried swears to marry Odette and never love another, but Von Rothbart tricks him. The next night, an impostor, Odile, comes to Prince Siegfried's party and makes him think that *she* is Odette. The Prince publicly swears his love for the impostor—and Odette is doomed to be a swan forever. The two lovers vow to die together rather than live under Von Rothbart's evil spell. The spell is broken, and Siegfried and Odette are reunited in heaven.

One of my first roles—when I was not quite seven and just beginning my ballet training with Eva Lorraine—was as the black swan, Odile, in a children's production of *Swan Lake*. A photographer came to my teacher's studio as we were preparing for our recital, and a few months later his photographs turned up in *Dance Magazine*. Amazingly, my picture as the little black swan was on the cover. Looking at that cover today, I can still remember how I felt!

dance

magazine

august 1953
50 cents

When I was twenty years old and had just been made a soloist, American Ballet Theatre director Lucia Chase scheduled me to dance Odette–Odile in *Swan Lake* for the very first time. When she told me, I was struck with terror and delight. American Ballet Theatre was then performing at the Shrine Auditorium in Los Angeles, where as a child I had watched the Royal Ballet perform *Swan Lake*. My performance would be at a Saturday matinee in the San Francisco Opera House. When the company had first performed its new production of *Swan Lake* a few months earlier, I had watched rehearsals as a fifth understudy. Now I was to dance it in two short weeks!

I had a wonderful partner, Gayle Young, and our coach, Dimitri Romanoff, had depth of experience and exquisite taste. The two weeks slipped by quickly, with me aching and exhausted from rehearsals. Finally, we reached San Francisco and the day of my performance—my big chance, if I could be ready for it.

On the day of the matinee, my dressing room table was piled high with small gifts—good-luck tokens for my debut. I hardly had time to think about what was going to happen, and then I was on stage as the Swan Queen, Odette. Crowded in the wings, the other dancers spurred me on with their good wishes. In the audience were my old friends from the San Francisco Ballet, where I had been a scholarship student; my parents, aunts, and cousins; and my favorite grammar-school teacher, Sister Dorothy, who had told me years before that I would dance my way to heaven.

My first performance of *Swan Lake* seems like a blur to me now but it was a success, and I was on my way to becoming the ballerina I had hoped to be one day.

The dual role that I dance, Odette–Odile, is the pinnacle of the prima ballerina's art, the role in which a ballerina is judged as a successor to all of the ballerinas who have danced it before her. It is my favorite role, in my favorite ballet.

Tonight I will dance in American Ballet Theatre's production of *Swan Lake* in New York City.

Today, a *Swan Lake* performance day, I wake up with butterflies in my stomach. I am still nervous before a performance, even after decades of performing. I think this feeling actually helps me to transform myself into the person I must be on the stage.

This will be a long day. To calm myself and to relax my muscles—stiff and aching from yesterday's rehearsal—I soak for about twenty minutes in a warm whirlpool bath while reading a new spy novel.

Then my three-year-old son, Lloyd, and I eat our breakfast together —cereal, eggs, toast, and orange juice, plus coffee for me and milk for Lloyd.

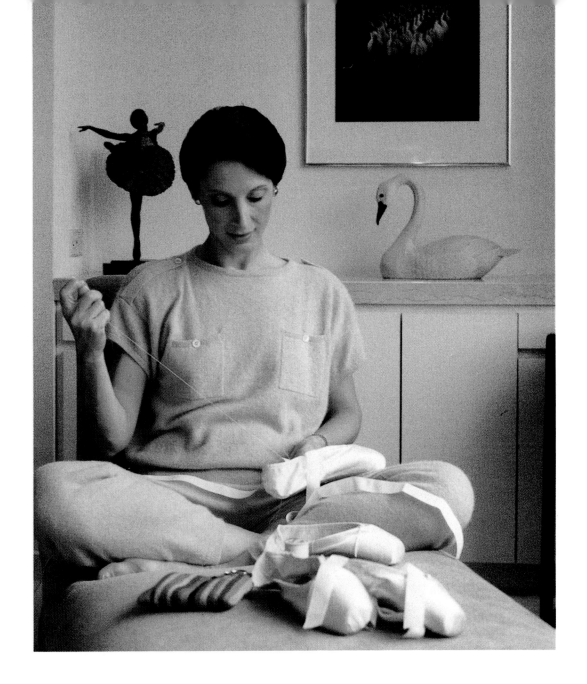

I decide to sew the ribbons and elastics on one more pair of pointe shoes so that when I go to class and rehearsal, I will be able to break them in. After all these years of performing, by now I must have sewn more than four thousand pairs of pointe shoes! I would never dream of letting anyone else do it for me. Every dancer has a special way of sewing the ribbons on her shoes so that they are just right for her own feet.

Next, I prepare for ballet class. Dancers take classes five or six times a week. It is the way we stay in good shape and keep our technique clean and strong.

American Ballet Theatre has a company class at the Metropolitan Opera House. Today, though, I am taking class with my favorite teacher, Wilhelm Burmann, at a studio on Broadway. Class starts at 10:30 A.M.

We start class holding on to the barre. We use it as a partner, holding on to it with our hands as we balance and turn. After about forty minutes at the barre, we go to the center of the room where we dance, watching ourselves in a mirrored front wall. In the mirror we can see what we do wrong (yes, I still make mistakes), and we can see what it looks like when we fix the mistakes. We must also *feel* what it feels like to fix our own mistakes, since we don't have a mirror when we are on stage.

Willi has a keen eye and he has helped me a lot with my jetés (jumps). On this day, Willi's corrections help and I begin to overcome my nervousness.

By the end of class, around noon, I am tired and sweaty. It feels as if I have already done a full day's work, but my day has barely begun. I take a cab from class to the Metropolitan Opera House.

As a ballerina, I am constantly in the public eye. Newspapers and magazines want to interview me, and TV and radio talk shows want me to appear in person. It is important for me to be part of this process, because the companies that present me want to use my name and reputation to draw audiences.

Today, as is often the case on a performance day, I have set aside a half hour in my dressing room to talk to a dance critic by telephone. I try to be as open and honest as I can. Still, like everyone else, I have to be tactful when talking to the press.

Often the magazine or newspaper sends along a photographer. Today I am lucky. The interview is by phone, and the newspaper will use stock photographs, so I'm spared another change of clothes and makeup.

After my interview, May Ishimoto, the company's wardrobe mistress, comes to my dressing room with my black swan costume. It has some new trim, and I haven't worn it for a few months. May wants to make sure my costume still fits perfectly. I try it on for her, and she makes a few last-minute adjustments. Costumes have to be very sturdy to hold up during our strenuous performances; and at the same time they must look dazzling, like my black swan costume, or light, soft, and feminine, like my white swan costume.

After my fitting, the company has scheduled a final studio rehearsal for my cast before the performance. Stage time is in very short supply, and usually I don't have more than a few rehearsals on stage during an entire year.

American Ballet Theatre, like most ballet companies, has several different casts of principal dancers but only one corps de ballet—the body of the dance company—for each production. The members of the corps play the swan maidens (there are usually twenty-four of them), courtiers, and other roles without solo parts, dancing as an ensemble. The soloists have featured dances to perform (such as the dance for the two big swans in the second act, or the six princesses in the third act) but do not have starring roles in the production. The lead roles are played by principal dancers.

Our cast of principals, like the others, usually works as a unit. There is little switching of principal dancers between casts except in the event a leading dancer from another cast is injured. Unfortunately, injuries are a frequent occurrence—particularly among male dancers, who do a lot more jumping than ballerinas do and who also have to lift their partners. More than once I can remember having a performance cancelled because my partner hurt himself while substituting for an injured dancer in another cast. So, in addition to worrying about injuring myself, I am always worried about my partner injuring himself.

Rehearsals during a rehearsal period—but not on a performance day—can last all day, from 11:00 A.M. until 6:00 or 7:00 P.M., with only an hour's break for lunch. I use the time to break everything down and work step-by-step with the choreography. I learn to pace myself by finding the spots where I can relax and the spots where I must push hard, because in performance a ballerina must always look fresh and never show just how hard she is working.

A ballerina always looks like she is completely in control and could go on dancing forever, as if her feet never touched the ground. The audience comes to the ballet to be transported to another world—a world of perfect creatures who seem to float and to fly with no effort at all. Nothing could be farther from the truth. In order to achieve such an "out-of-this-world" effect, I must work very hard every day, for creating this illusion is the most difficult part of the ballerina's art.

Rehearsals on the day of a performance usually don't last more than a couple of hours. Today we will use our time to go over details and to work out a few problem areas in the choreography. I don't like to run completely through a ballet on the day of performance for two reasons: First, I don't want to exhaust myself before the evening performance; and second, I feel that the performance won't be fresh and spontaneous if it's *too* rehearsed.

In rehearsals, we almost always work to music played live on the piano. With live music, we can easily ask the pianist to change the tempo or to insert pauses for breathing—just as a conductor does during a real performance with orchestra. For *Swan Lake*, with my difficult second-act solo, we need a very experienced pianist, like Gladys Celeste, who is playing the piano for this rehearsal.

Today I'm working with Georgina Parkinson, the ballet mistress; my partner, Ross Stretton, who plays Prince Siegfried; and Michael Owen, who plays the evil Von Rothbart. Ross has danced as Prince Siegfried with me many times. He is a wonderful dancer, very elegant and pure in his style.

Georgina, who used to be a ballerina with Great Britain's Royal Ballet, has had years of experience with our roles. She knows the choreography completely, and she knows Ross and me, and all our strengths and weaknesses. Georgina corrects us a few times and gives us suggestions on how to use our arms.

If the ballet is new or is one that I haven't performed many times, or if the costumes are new, I like to put on the costume to see how it feels and works. My partner likes to get the feel of the costume and needs me to try out different turns and lifts so that he can learn how to work with it. If my costume is a big tutu (the name comes from the stiff, gauzelike material called tulle that is used to make the costume), my partner cannot see my feet and must dance with me from a bit farther away. He needs to practice doing that. If I have to wear a long skirt or a heavy one, we must try turns to see if the costume gets in the way or slows the speed of the turn.

Once, when I was making my debut in a new version of *Swan Lake*, there was no dress rehearsal for me. During the first performance, just as I was making my entrance, my crown caught in some mesh on one of the sets. Fortunately, after a few seconds of flapping my swan wings, the crown came free by itself.

Our rehearsal on this performance day is nearly over. We finish at about 2:00 P.M., and I'm ready for lunch. I need to eat enough so that I will have energy left for the last act of *Swan Lake*, which doesn't start until 10:30 P.M.

At home for lunch, I make myself an omelette and a salad. I eat my lunch with Lloyd, who shares my vanilla milk shake. After lunch comes my quiet time—a couple of hours of reading, playing the piano, napping, and just resting for the night ahead. I need this time to free my mind and body for the upcoming performance. I must be as refreshed and as relaxed as possible before going to the theater.

For an 8:00 P.M. curtain, I must be at the theater at least two hours ahead of time. Even though I don't appear in the first act of *Swan Lake*, there are many preparations for a full-length ballet. I leave home in a comfortable dress (I'm going to come back later to change for a dinner party), and I kiss my son good-bye.

At 5:45 P.M., I arrive by taxi at the stage door of the Metropolitan Opera House. There are a few ballet fans who are waiting to greet me and wish me luck for the evening ahead. I go in the stage door and write my initials next to my name on the sign-in sheet. This lets the stage manager know that I'm in the theater for the performance.

Then I go to my dressing room, where I spend at least the next hour preparing myself for the performance. My dressing room is the one place I can relax in privacy. Everything I need is set out: makeup, hairpins, brush and comb, dance clothes, shoes, cold cream, perfume, hair spray, sweaters and shawls—and lots of little good-luck trinkets, cards, and photographs to make it feel like home. I keep all my things in the same places I have used for years so that I can find something instantly even in a new theater.

First, I get out of my street clothes and into comfortable sweat pants and a tee-shirt. I put soft ballet slippers on my feet and then sit down at the dressing table to apply my makeup. For *Swan Lake*, I must put a very light—almost white—pancake makeup on my face and on my complete upper body. On stage, I am supposed to be a woman who has been turned into a swan by an evil magician, so my body must look white, like the white feathers of the swan. I am always careful not to get a suntan. If you are brown from the sun and you apply white body makeup, it looks purple under the blue lights.

Stage makeup must be very exaggerated so that even the people sitting in the last rows of the theater are able to see the performers' features. For *Swan Lake*, I want my eyes to look large, dark, and slightly slanted, so I put long, feathery false eyelashes on the tops and bottoms of my eyelids and draw strong black lines past the outside corners of my eyes. I use brown and peach blush to contour my cheeks, cheekbones, forehead, and chin. For different roles, I use different colored eye shadows and lipsticks. Tonight I will use blues, pinks, and silvery-white eye shadows and a clear coral-red lipstick.

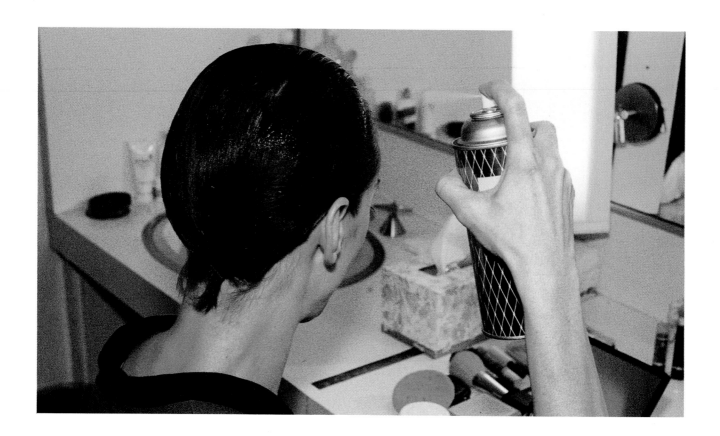

When I have finished my makeup and checked my pointe shoes, I fix my hair. I have short hair, but when I perform, I slick it back with gel, put an invisible hair net over it, and attach a false bun to my head with lots of strong, steel hairpins. Then I spray it with hair spray. When it dries, it feels like a helmet, but it will stay in place for the whole performance.

Once my hair is done, it is time to put on my feathered headpiece and crown. The white feathers curl around my ears and are tied with a ribbon that I hide under my bun. The crown sparkles with rhinestones, crystals, and pearls. I look in the mirror at my huge dark eyes and smooth white face, arms, neck, and chest. As I begin to look like the character I'll be dancing, I begin to feel like the tragic Odette, trapped in the body of a swan. This helps me to prepare for the illusion I'll be creating; for when I step out on stage, I must become that character.

Over the loudspeaker in my room, I hear the orchestra warming up. Outside my door, noise and activity are increasing as the time for the performance nears. I pull on my leg warmers, slip a shawl around my shoulders, and leave my room to go warm up.

Backstage there are portable barres where we do our warm-ups before the performance. I do my own series of exercises developed through the years, things that work best for me; and even though I could do my exercises anywhere, I have a favorite spot that I always use. My warm-up usually takes around a half hour. By the time I am finished, I am dripping wet.

In my dressing room, I pull off my wet things and put on my pink tights and ballet trunks, more leg warmers, and my favorite robe. I bought my robe in Cleveland in 1977, and I have worn it for every performance since then. I think it brings me good luck.

Once again I check everything. My two pairs of pointe shoes are clean, powdered, and ready to go. I need two pairs because, after being worn in the second act, the first pair gets too soft from perspiration to be used in the rest of the performance. Both my white swan (second act) and black swan (third act) tutus are hanging up, and my crown for the third act is on the table ready to be pinned on. My body is creamy white and warmed up, my nerves are in check, and the first act is about to begin.

I don't appear in the first act, but I run out on stage to wish Ross luck. Dancers do this the way actors tell each other to "break a leg." I watch about half of the first act from the wings and start to put on my pointe shoes.

Putting on my shoes is a complicated process. I have to make sure they will stay on my feet and that the ribbons, after they are tied around my ankles, are tucked in securely. There is a tub of water and a box of chunky, powdery rosin on both sides of the stage. Sitting near the rosin box, I dip the heels and ribbons of my pointe shoes in the water and rub the heels of my feet in the rosin. Then I wrap my toes in a layer of paper towel and put on the shoes. The water and rosin mixture form a glue that will make the heel of my shoe stay on securely. I wrap the ribbons once around my arch and once around my ankle and tie a firm knot. Then I put rosin on the wet tips of the ribbons and tuck them in tightly. Again the glue makes sure that I won't have any loose ribbons dangling. My shoes are pink like my tights; for the second act of *Swan Lake*, I put a light dusting of white powder and rosin on the shoes. It makes my foot and leg look like one long line because the shoe fades right into the tights and becomes almost invisible.

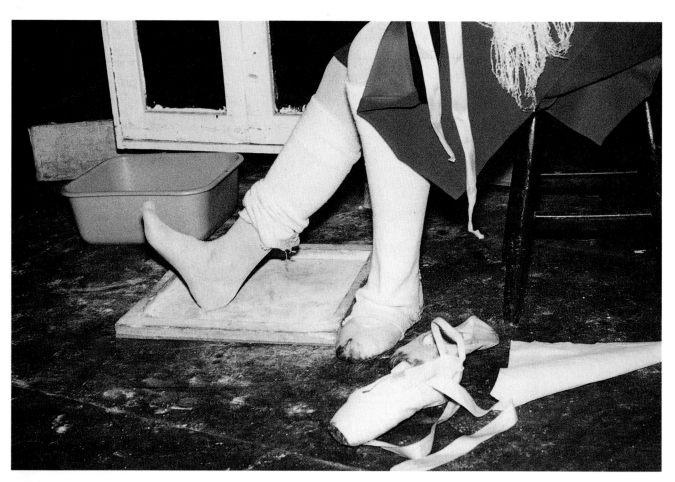

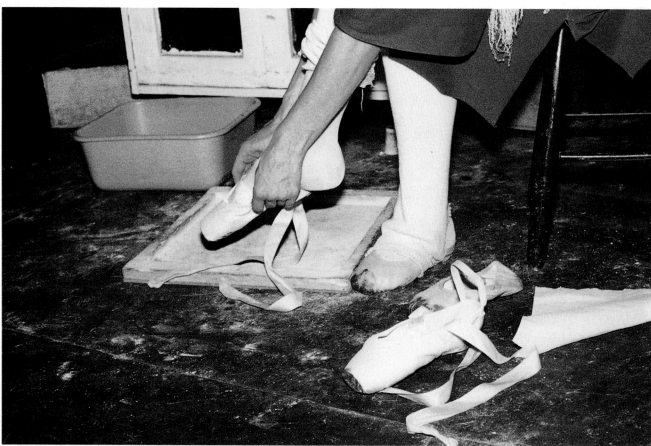

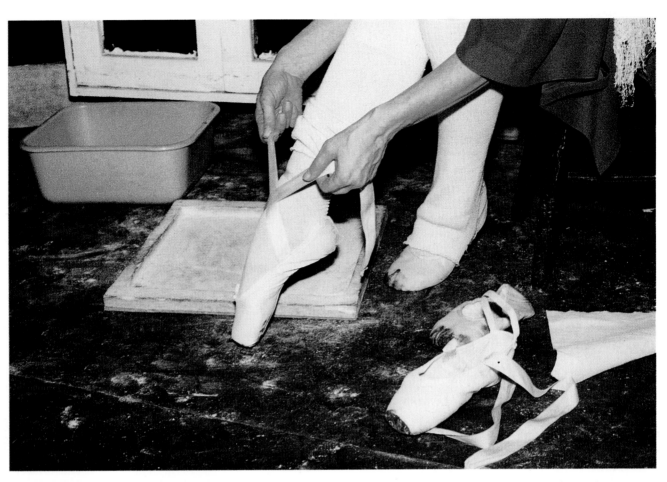

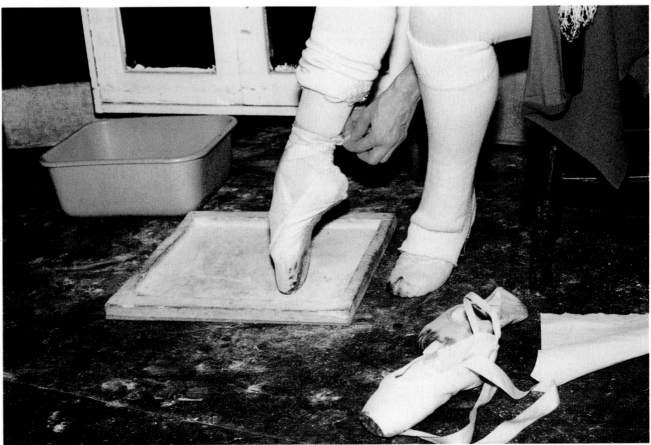

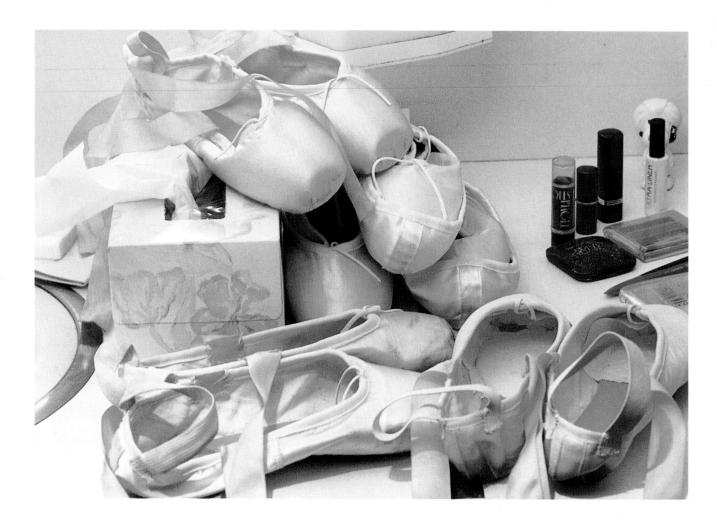

Before going back to my dressing room to put on my costume for the second act, I watch the pas de trois (dance for three) in the first act. Two soloists are dancing it with a new male principal dancer, and they are giving a beautiful performance. I applaud them from the wings as the first act is nearing its close.

Quickly I pull on my white tutu, give a last-minute check to my makeup and hair, and blow a kiss to the photograph of my son. I still have on one pair of leg warmers as I go back out onstage to try a few of the more difficult steps. This last-minute practice warms me up and helps me to work out the jitters.

The orchestra conductor watches me try a few steps so that he will know how to follow me. Unlike opera and symphonic music, in ballet it is not the conductor but the ballerina who sets the tempo of the music for her solos.

The stage is now set. It is an enchanted forest with a glittering lake and castle in the background. The stagehands are making last-minute adjustments to the lights, and the stage is filling up with all the corps de ballet in their white swan costumes. Everyone is trying out steps or checking shoe ribbons when, suddenly, the stage manager, Alice Galloway, calls out, "Places, please!" It's up to her to keep the show moving smoothly. We file into the wings, take off our leg warmers, step in and out of the rosin box, and wait for the music to begin and the curtain to go up.

As my cue in the music nears, I step into the wing from which I will make my first entrance. My heart is pounding, my hands are icy, and my legs feel weak; but I bravely make my leap out onto the stage. The ice is broken! The audience applauds my entrance, and my performance begins.

As soon as I am on the blue-lit stage, I am Odette, alone in the forest and frightened when I first see Prince Siegfried with his bow and arrow. Our eyes meet, and my fright turns into fascination. It's love at first sight for both of us. I tell him my tragic story—that I am Odette, Queen of the Swans—using not words but mime. Siegfried bows but mimes that he does not understand. I point to the lake filled, I mime, with my mother's tears. My mother wept because Von Rothbart changed me into the Swan Queen; under Von Rothbart's spell, I will always be a swan, except between the hours of midnight and dawn, unless a man swears his love for me, marries me, and never loves another.

Siegfried swears his love for me, and we forget all else as we dance together. As the second act finishes, the dawn is breaking. I am transformed from a young woman into a swan once again. Von Rothbart drags me from my handsome young prince. Siegfried watches as I fly away, and he is left alone as the curtain falls.

I thank my partner for the second act. Back in my dressing room, I rest a bit and then change into my third-act costume. May Ishimoto, the wardrobe mistress, stops at my dressing room to check the black swan costume one last time.

In the second and fourth acts of *Swan Lake*, I am the sad and lovely white swan, Odette. But in the third act I am Von Rothbart's evil creation: the glittering, alluring black swan, Odile. In both roles, I must give the impression of being a swan—my arms must move with the smooth, graceful, elegant flow of wings. As Odile, I must also be strong and sharper in my movements. I must believe in what I'm doing, so that the audience will be able to believe it, too.

In the third act, Odile is presented at Prince Siegfried's grand ball by Von Rothbart. Michael Owen has been playing Von Rothbart in my cast of principal dancers for many years. In the second and fourth acts, when I play Odette, Von Rothbart is my captor and tormentor. In the third act, however, when I am the evil Odile, he is my conspirator in trying to trick Prince Siegfried, and he gives me an extra dose of evil inspiration.

At the ball, the Queen has gathered six beautiful princesses from among whom Siegfried is to select his bride. The lovesick Prince dances with each princess but doesn't choose any of them. Odile makes her entrance to the party with thunder booming and lightning flashing so the audience knows that something evil is about to happen.

The Prince is enchanted. In the role of Odile, I impersonate Odette by using subtle changes in my arms and facial expressions. As Odile and the Prince dance, he becomes certain that Odile is Odette at her most dazzling.

Before the third-act black swan pas de deux (dance for two), I am anxious and prancing around backstage near Alice Galloway's command post. She hears me sighing a lot—a big *huhhhh!* She tells me that I always give my best performances when I sigh the most.

The pas de deux that we do in this act is one of the most difficult and exciting in all of ballet, and the audience always looks forward to it. Near the end of the dance, I do thirty-two fouettés—complete turns on pointe on my left leg while my right leg is whipping in and out at hip height. I must try to stay in one spot as I do this, while the music builds to a climax. At the end of the black swan pas de deux, the audience thunders its approval. In over twenty years of dancing *Swan Lake*, I have never missed one of my thirty-two fouettés. I am proud of that record, because it comes from a lot of hard work.

At the end of act three, Prince Siegfried, completely beguiled, asks to marry Odile. As he swears his love to her, a vision of poor Odette floats at the back of the stage. Prince Siegfried is shocked and ashamed that Odile has tricked him. Von Rothbart and Odile disappear in a puff of smoke. As the curtain falls, Siegfried runs out of the castle to find Odette.

Dripping wet and exhausted, I return to my dressing room to change quickly back into my still-damp white tutu and feathers. I touch up my white body makeup and powder my pointe shoes once again. I am feeling some relief because the hardest part of the ballet is over.

My heart is still pounding and my head is abuzz with all the steps that either went extremely well or not as well as I would have liked. I strive for perfection and sometimes, on a good day, I can come pretty close. But in a ballet as long as *Swan Lake*, there are always parts that I'd like to do over again if I could.

The fourth act begins with the swan maidens lamenting their betrayal by Prince Siegfried. With Siegfried's third-act promise to marry Odile, the swans are now doomed to remain swans forever.

As Odette, I rush on stage in despair and mime that I will throw myself from the rocks into the lake to save the swan maidens from this terrible fate. Prince Siegfried comes running in and throws himself at my

feet to beg forgiveness. We join in a dance of hopeless love and vow to die together rather than live apart. It is a tragic ending, but the spell is broken. Von Rothbart is ruined and dies, and the beautiful swan maidens are saved. As the Tchaikovsky music builds and the curtain falls on the final act of *Swan Lake*, Prince Siegfried and I are reunited, sailing away to heaven on a magical swan boat.

Now, utterly exhausted but still flying high from the excitement of the performance, we take our bows. This is still part of the performance. I accept the bouquets of flowers, pluck a rose from one, and present it to Ross as a gesture of thanks and respect. The people in the audience leap to their feet and shout "Brava" for me and "Bravo" for Ross. We smile at each other and enjoy the moment.

With the curtain down, I can't wait to get out of my pointe shoes; but before I can, there are people to greet. Back in my dressing room, I finally climb out of my tutu and throw my favorite robe back on. I take off my shoes and sit down to catch my breath.

My dresser takes my wet tutus out of my dressing room and lets the first wave of well-wishers into the room. My husband, Hilary, is always the first person to enter; and he is beaming with pride. Amanda, my twelve-year-old stepdaughter, comes with him.

Then some friends and fellow dancers come in to congratulate me. People I haven't met before introduce themselves and their friends, and some ask me to autograph programs for themselves and for their children. Exhausted as I am, I am also gratified that these people have come to compliment me on the performance. As the crowd in my dressing room thins, I begin rubbing cold cream on my face, getting rid of the white skin and the huge eyes, and become my regular self again.

I wash my hair, shake it out and give it a comb, reapply some street makeup, and dress comfortably for the short ride home.

Hilary takes my dance bag, and I gather my flowers. I check the call-board to see at what time the next day's rehearsal is scheduled. Then I go out through the stage door to greet another group of fans. I sign more autographs and chat for a few minutes.

Our car is waiting, so we stow my things in the trunk and climb in. After a quick stop at home to change my clothes, our driver takes us off to a party in my honor at the Russian Tea Room, my favorite restaurant.

By the time I get there, it's after midnight on a day that started for me at 7:00 A.M. Everyone else has already arrived. The gentlemen are all formally dressed and the ladies are wearing fancy dresses. This is a special evening for us all.

As I enter the room, all the dinner guests stand and applaud, and I acknowledge the applause of my friends and fans.

At dinner, my colleagues and I toast each other for a job well done. By 1:30 A.M., we are ready to go home.

Back home, I look in on Lloyd and give my sleeping son a good-night kiss. I take off my makeup and get ready for bed. By the time my head hits the pillow, I am already asleep.

It's been a long day.

Milpitas Unified School District
Milpitas, California
Zanker School